The Princess Tales

The Princess Test

Gail Carson Levine
ILLUSTRATED BY Mark Elliott

HarperCollins*Publishers*

To Martha Garner,

who told me to be sweet.

—G.C.L.

The Princess Test
Text copyright © 1999 by Gail Carson Levine
Illustrations copyright © 1999 by Mark Elliott
All rights reserved. Manufactured in China.
For information address HarperCollins Children's Books,
a division of HarperCollins Publishers,
195 Broadway, New York, NY 10007.
http://www.harperchildrens.com

Library of Congress Cataloging-in-Publication Data
Levine, Gail Carson.
    The princess test / Gail Carson Levine ; illustrated by Mark
Elliott.
        p.   cm.
    "The princess tales."
    Summary: In this humorous retelling of Hans Christian
Andersen's "The Princess and the Pea," Lorelei must pass many
difficult tests in order to prove that she is a true princess and win
the hand of Prince Nicholas.
ISBN-10: 0-06-028062-X   ISBN-10: 0-06-028063-8 (lib. bdg.)
    [1. Fairy tales.]   I. Elliott, Mark, ill.   II. Andersen, H. C.
(Hans Christian), 1805-1875.   Prindsessen paa ærten.   III. Title.
PZ8.L4793Pr   1999   98-27960
[Fic]—dc21   CIP
                                                                  AC

Typography by Michele N. Tupper
19 SCP 21

First Edition

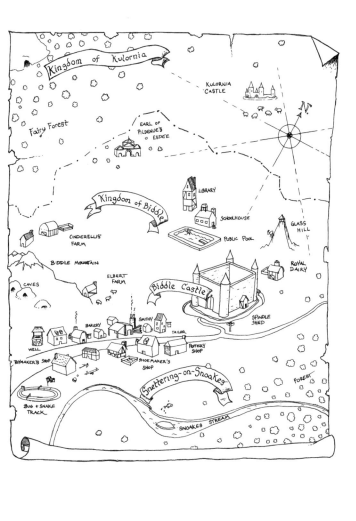

One

Once upon a time, in the village of Snettering-on-Snoakes in the Kingdom of Biddle, a blacksmith's wife named Gussie gave birth to a baby girl. Gussie and her husband, Sam, named the baby Lorelei, and they loved her dearly.

Lorelei's smile was sweet and her laughter was music. But as an infant she smiled only four times and laughed twice. The rest of the time she cried.

She cried when her porridge was too hot or too cold or too salty or too bitter or too sweet. She cried when her bath-water was too hot or too cold or too wet or not wet enough. She cried when her diaper was scratchy or smelly or not folded exactly right. She cried when her cradle was messy or when her mother forgot to make it with hospital corners. She cried whenever anything was not perfectly perfect.

Sam and Gussie did their best to make her happy. Lorelei was the only village baby with satin sheets and velvet diapers. She was the only one whose milk came from high-mountain yaks. And she was the only one who ate porridge made from two parts millet mixed with one part buckwheat. But still she cried.

She cried less as she learned to talk.

Then one day Lorelei said, "Father dearest and Mother dearest, I'm terribly sorry for crying so much. You have been too good to me."

Gussie said, "Oh honey, it's all right."

Sam said, "Gosh, we thought you were the cutest, best baby in this or any other kingdom."

Lorelei shook her head. "No, I was difficult. But I shall try to make it up to you. And now that I can explain myself, everything will be much better." She smiled. Then she sneezed. And sneezed again. She smiled shakily. "I fear I have a cold."

From then on, Lorelei stopped crying. She didn't stop being a picky eater, and she didn't stop needing everything to be just so. She just stopped crying about it.

Instead, Lorelei started being sick and having accidents.

If a child in the village of Snettering-on-Snoakes had a single spot, Lorelei caught the measles. If a child two villages and a mountain away had the

3

"SHE SMILED SHAKILY. 'I FEAR I HAVE A COLD.'"

mumps, Lorelei caught them, and the flu besides.

She loved the other children, and they liked her well enough. But if she played tag with them, she was sure to trip and skin her knee or her elbow or her chin. When they played hopscotch, she always twisted her ankle. Once, when she tried to jump rope, she got so tangled up that Gussie had to come and untie her.

When Lorelei turned fourteen, Gussie died. Sam and Lorelei were heartbroken. Sam swore never to marry again because Gussie was the sweetest wife anybody could ever have.

"Besides," he added, "all the old tales say that stepmothers are mean to their stepdaughters. You'll never have to worry about that, Lorelei honey."

Two

Sam knew that Lorelei couldn't cook and clean for him and be her own nurse too. Besides, he'd be leaving soon for his annual trip to shoe the horses of the Earl of Pildenue, and someone would have to take care of Lorelei while he was gone. So he looked around for a housekeeper.

A wench named Trudy had helped the shoemaker's family when their twins were born. The shoemaker said that Trudy was a hard worker, so Sam hired her. Trudy wondered why a black-smith with a grown daughter needed a housekeeper, but she took the job.

As soon as Trudy walked in the door, Lorelei ran to her, stumbled, and fell into Trudy's arms.

"Dear Trudy, I'll do anything to help you. To the outer limits of my meager ability."

Nobody had ever called Trudy "dear" before. So she thought this could be a pretty cushy spot, even if she understood only one word in ten that the lass said. But then again, if the girl wanted to help, why were the dirty dishes piled as high as a horse's rear end? Trudy shrugged and pumped water into the sink. "Here, lass. You can start on these."

"Oh, good!" Lorelei took the soap and started to scrub a plate.

Trudy looked around for a mop.

"Oh dear," Lorelei said.

"What's amiss?"

Lorelei raised her arms out of the soapy water. Trudy was horrified. The girl's arms and hands were covered with a bright-red rash.

"Does this happen whenever you wash a dish?" Trudy asked.

"I don't know. I've never washed one before."

Never washed a dish! Her poor dead mother had let her get away with that? Had the woman mistaken her daughter for a princess?

"Mother kept the unguents and the bandages in the hutch," Lorelei said.

Trudy opened the hutch door. There were enough potions and herbs and simples to set up shop as a wisewoman.

"That one. There." Lorelei pointed to a big jar.

Trudy spread the salve over Lorelei's rash.

"It has to be wrapped in clean linen."
Lorelei pointed again.

Trudy wrapped up Lorelei's arms—
three times. The first time the bandages
were too tight. The next time they were
too loose. An hour passed before Lorelei
said they were just right.

At last! Trudy thought. Her majesty is
satisfied.

"The dressing has to be changed
every two hours," Lorelei said. "I'm sorry
to be such a bother."

Trudy frowned. It wasn't exactly her
highness's fault, but over an hour had
gone by and the dishes were still dirty.
The floor hadn't been mopped, and there
was a mountain of laundry in the basket.
She'd be working half the night to get it
all done.

Trudy worked half the night that night and every night. For a month she took off bandages and put on bandages. When the rash was gone, Lorelei offered to help again.

Trudy hadn't been able to do any spinning because of all the bandaging. Surely, she thought, her majesty can't come to grief spinning. "Can you help me with the spinning?"

Lorelei smiled happily. Gussie had never let her near the spinning wheel. She knew exactly what to do, though, because she'd watched her mother so often. She sat down at the wheel and got started.

Trudy nodded. There. She began to dust.

"Oh dear."

Trudy turned around. Lorelei had stabbed herself in the hand with the spindle, and blood was pouring onto the cottage's wooden floor. Trudy ran for the bandages.

While Trudy bandaged her, Lorelei apologized at least a thousand times. After that, Trudy spent an hour scrubbing blood off the wooden floor and wondering what the bungling ninny was good for.

Not much, Trudy soon discovered. Lorelei could hang laundry on the line, and she could make a bed neatly. But the only thing she was really good at was embroidery. And Trudy had no need for embroidery. What she needed was to scream, long and loud.

Every day Trudy got madder and madder. While she washed Lorelei's satin sheets, her ladyship would be sitting at her ease, embroidering by the window. As Trudy kneaded Lorelei's special millet-buckwheat bread, the lazy thing would be lying in bed because her poor little throat hurt. Or her poor little left eyebrow. Or her poor little big toe.

Then came the joyous moment when Trudy thought of doing Lorelei in. Cooking her highness's goose. Rubbing her pampered self o-u-t. *Out!* Trudy started whistling.

Lorelei looked up from embroidering the outline of a potato on one of Sam's breeches. She smiled. "I'm so glad you're happy here, Trudy."

"Oh, I am, lass, I am. Happier every minute."

Three

It was lunchtime in the nearby court of the king and queen of Biddle. Queen Hermione rang her little bell to let the Royal Servants know they could bring out the first course.

The Chief Royal Lunchtime Serving Maid carried a platter heaped with crab cakes into the royal dining room. King Humphrey helped himself to a tiny crab cake. Queen Hermione helped herself to a tiny crab cake. Prince Nicholas took a dozen or so crab cakes and started eating.

King Humphrey tasted his crab cake. Queen Hermione tasted her crab cake. They shook their heads. Queen Hermione rang her bell again. The Chief Royal Lunchtime Serving Maid stepped up to the royal table.

"I'm so sorry," Queen Hermione said. "These crab cakes taste a bit too fishy to me."

"We beg to differ or disagree," the king boomed. "They're not fishy enough."

"Crab isn't a fish," Prince Nicholas said, chewing happily. "My compliments to the chef."

"Please bring grapefruit instead," the queen said.

The Chief Royal Lunchtime Serving Maid removed the platter. On her way into the kitchen she passed a counter where the royal lunch was laid out. There were platters of crusty beef Wellington, creamed potatoes, and asparagus in mustard sauce, and there was a basket of poppy seed popovers. And two plates of grapefruit sections, poached eggs, and dry toast.

At a long table the Royal Servants waited for their lunch. The Chief Royal Lunchtime Serving Maid handed the platter of crab cakes to the Chief Royal Steward at the head of the table. He took four or five cakes and passed the plate to the Chief Royal Housekeeper on his right.

"There would be more for us if the prince didn't eat so much," the Chief Royal Undergardener complained.

"Hush," the Chief Royal Housekeeper said. "We're lucky to serve two such finicky rulers. My cousin Mabel doesn't fare half so well at the Earl of Pildenue's castle. The earl and his family adore their food, adore their clothes, adore their furniture. She never gets anything."

⚓ ⚓ ⚓

Back in Snettering-on-Snoakes, Lorelei
ate her lunch of grapefruit, poached eggs,
and dry toast, and patted her mouth with
an embroidered napkin. Then she went
out to hang embroidered laundry on the
embroidered clothesline.

While she worked, she thought about
her mother and Trudy. Her mother had
been so good to her. And Trudy was
too. They both worked so hard. She
hadn't helped her mother much, or Trudy,
even though she always wanted to.

Trudy looked tired sometimes, although
she never complained. Gussie must have
been tired too. But no matter how tired
she might have been, her mother had
always had a kiss and a hug for Lorelei.
And even if the hugs had made Lorelei
a little black and blue, she would have
given anything to have them back again.

She wiped away a tear with the embroidered toe of Sam's hose.

Prince Nicholas, riding by, saw the tear. He had gone out after lunch to get some fresh air. As soon as he had turned into the lane, he'd seen Lorelei. She looked pretty in the distance. As he got closer, she was still pretty. Not a raving beauty, but definitely pretty. Light-brown hair. Ordinary color, but thick and wavy. Nose a little too big. But her eyes were big too. Enormous. And she had roses in her cheeks. You didn't see roses in the cheeks of the noble and stuck-up ladies at court.

Then he saw she was crying! A corner of his heart that had never been touched before was touched. He leaped off his steed. "Maiden!" he cried. "You weep!"

Lorelei turned and knocked over the laundry basket. Embroidered petticoats and tunics and bodices danced across the small muddy yard.

Prince Nicholas vaulted over the low fence and helped Lorelei gather up the wash. He picked up one of Sam's shirts, embroidered with three-legged stools. The stitchery was masterful. But why three-legged stools?

He asked, "Maiden, why were you crying? Perhaps I can be of service."

Lorelei blushed. He wasn't that handsome, but there was something regal about him. Who was he? "I was missing my mother, kind sir."

"Your mother is . . ."

"She died." Lorelei smiled bravely and gathered up the last item of laundry, a petticoat embroidered with tiny teakettles.

The poor maiden was an orphan, Nicholas thought. Or half of one if her

"LORELEI TURNED AND KNOCKED OVER
THE LAUNDRY BASKET."

father was alive. "You have my most sincere sympathy, maiden." He wanted to say more but couldn't think of anything else.

Lorelei smiled. "Thank you, kind sir." He was nice!

She had a wonderful smile. He found himself stammering. "Er . . . I am P-Prince N-Nicholas."

He was a prince! She swept him a curtsy. "I am Lorelei."

Inside, Trudy glanced up from her washtub. Look at her highness out there, she thought, passing the time with a young lord. Not for long, your ladyship. She hummed and danced a little jig. Not for long, hey-ho! Not for long, tra-la!

Four

When Nicholas got back to the castle, King Humphrey summoned him to the throne room. As usual it was full of courtiers and subjects. King Humphrey had just settled an argument between two farmers over a cow. When he saw Nicholas, the king ordered everyone to leave. The only ones left were the king, the queen, the prince, and the Chief Royal Window Washer, who was cleaning the stained-glass windows.

"Son," King Humphrey boomed. "We are growing old or advancing in years.

We should like to abdicate. But before we do, you must wed or get married."

Nicholas thought of Lorelei and his heart started to race. "I just met—"

"We must find you a true princess," Queen Hermione interrupted. "The descendent of a long line of royalty. A noble maiden, with . . ."

That eliminates Lorelei, Nicholas thought. Her pretty, rosy cheeks alone would rule her out.

"We've devised a test," the king said. "Or an examination."

"But what if I don't love the true princess?"

"You'll love her," Queen Hermione said. "She'll be just right for you."

No she won't! thought Nicholas.

"You'll make yourself love or adore her," King Humphrey roared. "Or we'll abdicate in favor of Archduke Percival."

Nicholas hated the archduke. Percy threw his servants into the moat if they did something wrong or if he felt like it. He would be a terrible king.

"Would you like to hear the test, dear?" the queen asked.

Nicholas nodded.

"When a maiden arrives who claims to be a true princess," Queen Hermione said, "we shall give her a bouquet."

The king guffawed. "But amidst all the fragrant or sweet-smelling flowers, there will be a sprig or small bunch of parsley. And that's not a flower."

Nicholas wondered what parsley had to do with being a princess.

"The true princess will know," the queen said. "She will pluck that parsley right out of her bouquet."

"That's the test?"

"Certainly not," Queen Hermione said.

"There's more. We shall serve her a salad. A beautiful salad."

"Except," King Humphrey said, chuckling, "right in the middle, there will be a bit—"

"A speck—" the queen interrupted.

"The merest fleck. We don't want to hurt or injure the maiden. There will be a fleck of uncooked or raw noodle."

"The true princess will find it!" Queen Hermione announced.

What did parsley and noodles have to do with being a kind and just ruler? Nicholas listened in amazement to the rest of the test. There would be a trial in every course of the banquet. Also, the poor princess would be given a gown with a skirt that was a tint lighter than the bodice. She'd have to notice. She'd be shown a tapestry and would have to find the single missing stitch.

Lorelei might pass that one, Nicholas thought.

Every inch of the princess would be measured. Her waist had to be tiny. Her hands and feet had to be small, although her fingers had to be long. Her big toe had to be longer than her index toe. She had to be tall, but not a giant. And so on.

"But the final test will be the most important one," Queen Hermione said.

"There's more?" Nicholas said.

King Humphrey nodded solemnly. Then he nodded again.

"She will sleep in a guest bedroom," the queen said. "Her bed will be piled with twenty soft mattresses."

"She'll fall off!" Nicholas said. "She'll hurt—"

"A princess does not fall," the queen said. She went on. "Each mattress will be filled with the finest swans' feathers. But

25

under the bottom mattress we will place a pea. If she sleeps well, she is no true princess!"

King Humphrey agreed. "If she sleeps or slumbers well, she is no true princess!"

⚓ ⚓ ⚓

The Chief Royal Chambermaid heard about the pea test from the Chief Royal Window Washer. It made her curious, so she got a pea from the Chief Royal Cook. A dried pea, because they couldn't have meant a fresh one, which would just squoosh flat.

The Chief Royal Chambermaid made everything ready, just as it would be for the princess. One pea. Twenty mattresses. And a ladder.

She climbed up. The bed was sooo soft. It was delicious. Pea? She couldn't feel any pea. With twenty mattresses under her, she doubted she would feel a watermelon. She didn't think anybody could feel the pea—true princess, fake princess, or any other kind.

The Chief Royal Chambermaid climbed down and yanked off a few mattresses. Then she climbed back up. She still couldn't feel the pea. She pulled off more mattresses and tried again. Nothing.

She took off all the mattresses except the bottom one, but she still couldn't feel anything. She checked under the mattress. There it was. Well, she was no princess. Maybe a true princess could feel a pea under one or two mattresses. But under twenty? Not on your life.

Five

$\mathcal{S}$am got ready for his trip to the earldom of Pildenue. The earl was his only
noble customer. Sam made enough from
this one job to keep Lorelei in silk kirtles
and embroidery thread for a year.

He said a long farewell to Lorelei in
front of their cottage. "Be sure you wear
your shawl at night, honey."

"I will, Father."

"Be sure she does, Trudy. I don't want
her to get sick."

"Yes, Master," Trudy said. Would that
be a good way to bump her off? Let her
catch cold and die?

"And make her eat enough, Trudy. You have to keep your strength up, sweetie pie."

"Yes, Master," Trudy said. Should she starve Lorelei? No. It would take too long.

"Here, sweet. Give your old daddy a kiss."

Lorelei hugged him. "I'll miss you, Father. Hurry home."

Sam climbed up to the seat of his wagon. He flapped the reins, and the old mare started to trot.

Lorelei wiped away a tear. She turned to Trudy. "We'll just have to keep each other company." She sniffled. "We'll have a lovely time, won't we?"

"Yes, lass." Yes indeed!

⚓ ⚓ ⚓

King Humphrey wrote a proclamation

to announce the search for a real princess.

"Hear ye! Hear ye! Or listen well! Insofar and Inasmuch as We, King Humphrey, Supreme Ruler and Monarch of the Kingdom and Monarchy of Biddle . . ."

The king paused here. But there was no synonym for Biddle, so he went on.

". . . Wish to Abdicate Our Throne in Favor of Our Son and Heir, the Noble and Royal Prince Nicholas. And Insofar and Inasmuch as We Stipulate and Require . . ."

And so on. The next important part came at the very end. ". . . and Said Princess Must Satisfy Us, King Humphrey, Supreme . . ." Blah blah blah. ". . . That She Is in Her Person and Her Self a Completely and Utterly True Princess. Our Judgment on This Matter or in This Respect Shall be Final and Without Appeal."

Below that King Humphrey signed *King Humphrey or Supreme Ruler of Biddle*, as was his habit. The Royal Seal was affixed, and the proclamation was complete. And finished, too.

Except for one thing. The king wanted a portrait of Prince Nicholas to go with the proclamation. He sent for his Chief Royal Artist and Portrait Maker.

"My son or heir isn't a bad-looking boy, is he?" King Humphrey asked the artist. "There's nothing wrong with his looks, is there?"

"Oh no, Sire. Not in the slightest." The Chief Royal Artist and Portrait Maker thought the prince was ordinary-looking. Nothing special.

"The prince has to look handsome in his portrait or picture," the king said.

"That way a true princess will want and desire to come."

"I understand, sire." Smaller ears. Straighter mouth. Broader shoulders. He could do that.

Nicholas wanted to look as ugly as possible in his portrait. He wanted every princess who saw it to say, "Ugh. Who would want to marry *him*?" Because if no princesses showed up, he might be able to convince the king and queen to let him marry Lorelei.

So he squinted. He squirmed. He mussed his hair. He let his mouth hang open. He drooled. He borrowed Queen Hermione's makeup and drew a big black mole on his chin.

It made no difference. The Chief Royal Artist and Portrait Maker was a master craftsman. In the portrait Prince Nicholas' chin (without a mole) was lifted

"THE SEARCH WAS ON."

majestically. His eyes had a piercing look. A hint of a smile played around his mouth. His shoulders were broad. His mouth wasn't lopsided. His ears were perfect. Also, the Chief Royal Artist and Portrait Maker waved Nicholas' hair and thickened his eyelashes. Princesses would fall in love with those eyelashes. Guaranteed.

When all was ready, scribes copied the proclamation. Lesser Royal Artists and Portrait Makers copied the portrait. Messengers were dispatched to kingdoms near and far.

The search was on.

Six

Trudy thought about how to do Lorelei in. She could hit her over the head with the frying pan. Or strangle her with the embroidered clothesline. Or drag her to the village square and push her out of the clock tower. Any one of those would be lots of fun. But she'd be caught. The dopey villagers liked Lorelei.

It should be easy to finish her off, Trudy reasoned. After all, her highness was in bed sick or hurt three times a week without anybody doing anything to her. Why, she could murder herself one of these days without Trudy's having to lift a finger! Hmm. Now that was an idea.

The morning after Sam left, Trudy announced that she didn't feel well. "You'll have to do the housework today, lass," Trudy said. "I'm not up to it."

Lorelei would wash the dishes and she'd get that rash again. But today Trudy would be too sick to put on the salve. So Lorelei would swell up like a balloon and *POP!* And nobody would think it was Trudy's fault.

"Oh dear. Does your stomach ache?"

Trudy nodded.

"Oh dear. Does your forehead pulse?"

Trudy nodded.

"Your throat. Is it hard to swallow?"

Trudy nodded.

Lorelei clapped her hands. "Then I know just what to do. You've been so good to me, dear Trudy. And now I can help you." She threw open the door to the hutch and pulled out strangely shaped bottles and odd bundles of herbs.

"I used to get what you have," Lorelei said. "Mother made me well in a jiffy." She dumped whatever was in the bottles and bundles into a pot. Then she hung the pot on a hook in the fireplace.

Soon a sharp odor filled the room. Trudy's eyes watered. The hairs in her nose felt like they were burning.

"Doesn't it smell wonderful?" Lorelei asked. "I always feel better when I smell the steam. In a few minutes you'll drink the broth and be well again, dear Trudy."

She was going to have to *drink* that slop? Trudy jumped up. "I feel much better. Fine. Really." She poured the disgusting brew on the fire. Stinky smoke billowed out. "You're a good wisewoman.

You've cured me already." Trudy opened the cottage door and the windows. She could have been killed!

She started on the chores. What else could she do? Hmm. "Lass?"

"Yes, Trudy?"

"I'm off to the market. While I'm gone, would you like to try the spinning wheel again?"

"Oh yes!"

"I won't be long. Be careful with the spindle." Trudy shut the door behind her and sauntered down the lane. Her ladyship would stab herself again. By the time Trudy got back, Lorelei would have bled to death.

The market was busy. Trudy gossiped with the other shoppers. She told the peddlers what was wrong with their goods. She even bought herself a pink hair ribbon. Then she strolled back to the blacksmith's cottage. What a delightful day it was!

She opened the door. No, it was a terrible day! Lorelei wasn't bleeding. Not even a drop. The only thing that was hurt was the spinning wheel. It looked like a giant spider had spun a web all over it. It would take days to untangle the mess.

Lorelei was crying. "Oh, Trudy! I'm sorry. I wanted to have yards and yards of beautiful linen finished when you got back. You must be so disappointed in me."

Lorelei couldn't understand what Trudy was saying. It sounded something like "Argul! Gloog! Blub!" Trudy yanked open the cottage door and slammed it behind her. She stood on the doorstep, panting. She had to get a grip on herself. She couldn't let that little . . . that little good-for-nothing fancy *idiot* do this to her.

She had to plan it out better. She had plenty of time. Two months before Sam came home. Plenty of time.

Lorelei was as good as dead.

Seven

A month went by and no one arrived at the court of Biddle to take the princess test. Queen Hermione smiled knowingly. She said the young ladies were getting ready, having gowns made, making themselves beautiful for their prince.

Making themselves as princessy as possible, Nicholas thought. I want Lorelei! He wanted to cry.

Every day he rode to her lane in the village of Snettering-on-Snoakes. He spent hours watching the smoke curl out of her chimney. He didn't even have to see her. Just seeing the smoke was enough.

But sometimes he did see her, sitting at her window, embroidering. He'd wonder what she was sewing. Buckets? Doorknobs? Galoshes? He thought his heart would break in two pieces.

One day Lorelei was outside, picking roses from the bush outside the cottage door. She turned when she heard the clatter of his horse's hooves. It was that nice prince again, she thought. What was his name? Nicholas. A nice name. She curtsied.

Nicholas jumped off his horse. He bowed. What could he say to her? "Er . . . hello. Er . . . hello, maid Lorelei."

She smiled. "Hello, Your Highness."

"Fine weather we're having." He wished he could think of something more interesting to say.

"I think the clouds mean rain." Why couldn't she think of something more interesting to say? He probably knew a hundred princesses who could make fascinating conversation.

"Those roses are pretty. Did you plant them?"

Inside the cottage Trudy was cleaning the stove. She saw Lorelei through the window and wished the sluggard would prick herself with a poisoned thorn. She wished that the young lord talking to Lorelei were a highwayman who would kidnap her. Then he'd have to clean up after her and bandage her. Then she'd be his problem.

Hmm ... Trudy thought, that's it! That's the way to get rid of her, once and for all.

⚓ ⚓ ⚓

The very next day a princess showed up at King Humphrey's court. She was Princess Cordelia from the nearby kingdom of Kulornia.

King Humphrey himself helped her down from her carriage.

She was good-looking. The king didn't have his tape measure with him, but she seemed tall enough. And her hands looked the right size.

Queen Hermione smiled. The maiden looked promising.

Prince Nicholas frowned and bowed. He could tell already. He didn't like Cordelia.

"Thank you." She curtsied. "Well, well, well. Here I am. We made good time getting here. We only stopped three times on the road. Traffic wasn't bad. Dandy courtyard you have here, Humphrey. Hello, Nicky. I see they exaggerated on your

44

portrait. I expected that, so don't worry about it. They always do it in the marriage game. Well, well. Dandy courtyard . . ."

Queen Hermione looked at her husband. They had forgotten to put in a test for the art of conversation.

King Humphrey looked at his wife. They had forgotten to put in a test for talking your head off or never shutting up.

Nicholas looked at the sky. Nicky! He mustn't scream. He didn't have to marry anybody yet.

The king snapped his fingers. The Chief Royal Bouquet Maker stepped forward. He presented a bouquet to Princess Cordelia.

Let her not find the parsley, Nicholas prayed.

Let her not find the parsley or herb, the king prayed.

Let her not find the parsley, the queen prayed.

"Well, well, well. You folks sure know how to roll out the red carpet. There's nothing like a bunch of flowers to brighten things up. Take a dull tower room and—"

"Would you like us to put them in water, my dear?" Queen Hermione asked. If she said yes, it would be all over.

"Sure. Wouldn't want them to go limp and croak right in—"

"We're so glad you had a comfortable journey," King Humphrey interrupted firmly. "We hope or desire that it will be even better going the other way. Thank you so much for coming." He handed her back into the carriage and slapped the horses to get them moving quickly or rapidly.

Princess Cordelia stuck her head out the window. "Well! What did I do? I thought we were getting along just fine. When you issue a . . ."

The three of them went back into the castle. They could hear Cordelia yelling till the heavy doors thudded shut behind them.

Eight

On the same day that the talkative Princess Cordelia was thrown out of Biddle, Trudy perfected her plan. She would lose Lorelei, plain and simple. And whoever found her would have to keep her—finders keepers. Trudy giggled.

"Lass," Trudy said. "What's the name of that herb you like in your tea sometimes?"

"Hyssop?"

"That's the one. We're fresh out of it, and there's none in the market."

"That's all right." Lorelei smiled bravely. "I can do without."

"But I don't want you to, sweet. I want you to be happy, honey lamb."

"You're so good to me."

Hah! "Tim, the spice peddler, told me where it grows in the forest. I thought we could harness your dad's mule and go there tomorrow. We'll have a picnic."

"What fun!"

Hooray! Trudy thought. The bumbling ninny would never find her way home from the middle of the forest.

⚓ ⚓ ⚓

The next day princesses arrived at the castle in droves. They came in carriages drawn by horses, by camels, by oxen. One even came in a carriage drawn by crocodiles. And another arrived in a hot-air balloon. The courtyard was clogged with animals and carriages and princesses. The Royal Guards got tired of raising and lowering the drawbridge. They decided to leave it lowered till the prince announced his engagement.

There were too many princesses to test one by one. So the king and queen decided to test them all together.

Nicholas looked them over. Some were too short. Some were too tall. Some were too thin. Some were too fat. They'd all fail the measurement test. But the rest seemed about right. The most beautiful princess was the one who'd come in the carriage pulled by crocodiles. She had huge purple eyes and a slow smile. She gave Nicholas the shivers. He kept feeling she didn't want to marry him—she really wanted to roast him and eat him with cream sauce.

In the forest Lorelei finished weaving a daisy chain. She was in a small clearing, sitting on an embroidered blanket, a velvet embroidered blanket, of course. The only kind that didn't make her itchy.

Trudy was hunting for hyssop, the herb for Lorelei's tea.

"Do you see any?" Lorelei called.

"Not yet. Eat your lunch. I'll be there soon."

Lorelei opened the picnic basket. Trudy's voice sounded faraway. Lorelei bit into her cucumber sandwich with the crusts cut off. "Trudy!" she called. "Come back. You must be hungry."

"Soon. I think I see something."

Lorelei could hardly hear the words. It was too bad that Trudy couldn't enjoy this beautiful day. The spice peddler should have drawn a map showing exactly where the hyssop grew. Lorelei finished her

51

"LORELEI FINISHED WEAVING A DAISY CHAIN."

lunch and leaned back on the blanket. Such sweet puffy white clouds. She closed her eyes. In a few minutes she was asleep.

Trudy led Leonard the mule along the trail next to the stream. Lorelei hadn't called in a while. It was safe to stop. Trudy tied Leonard to a tree and took the extra lunch out of his saddlebag. She kicked off her shoes and sat on a rock with her feet dangling in the cool water. She bit into her sandwich. Sausages and peppers. Her favorite. This was peace.

Prince Nicholas couldn't stand being around all these princesses for another minute. He saddled his horse and rode to Snettering-on-Snoakes. He had to see Lorelei.

But she wasn't there. Her cottage was empty.

⚓ ⚓ ⚓

The first drops of rain woke Lorelei. The sky was dark.

"Trudy?"

A roll of thunder drowned her out. The drops came down harder. They were huge.

"Trudy? Do you hear me?"

Had Trudy come back and eaten her lunch while she was asleep? Lorelei opened the basket. No. Trudy's sausage-and-peppers sandwich was still there. Trudy is lost! Lorelei thought. Poor Trudy. She must be terrified.

Lightning lit the sky. Were you supposed to get under a tree when there was lightning? Or stay away from trees?

At least she'd be drier under a tree. Lorelei jumped up and folded the blanket neatly. Then she took the picnic basket and ran under a tall maple.

She stayed under the tree for an hour. Every few minutes she called Trudy, but there was never an answer. The sky grew darker. Storm dark, but also night dark. Lorelei's stomach rumbled delicately. Time for dinner.

She had to find Trudy. It was her responsibility because she was Trudy's mistress. She had never felt so full of purpose before. She had to find Trudy and Leonard the mule and get them home safely. She'd go to the stream first. The last time she'd heard Trudy's voice, it had come from there.

The stream was across the clearing and straight ahead, through a stand of trees. Lorelei stepped into the clearing and was drenched instantly. Oh well, she thought. It was only water.

"Trudy! Stay where you are. I'm coming." She didn't want poor Trudy to have one second more of terror than she had to.

As the water soaked into them, Lorelei's skirts got heavier and heavier and dragged more and more. It was hard to walk, but she had to do it.

"Trudy! I'm coming!"

Where was the stream? She should have reached it by now.

"Leonard?" Maybe the mule would hee-haw and she'd find him. Then she could ride him and find Trudy more quickly. She pushed past bushes and over fallen logs.

Two hours passed. Lorelei still hadn't found Leonard, Trudy, or the stream. She was hungry and chilled. She sneezed almost as often as she took a breath. She couldn't get sick, not now when Trudy needed her.

Finally Lorelei sat on a tree stump and cried between sneezes. She had to admit it. Trudy was lost. Leonard was lost. And she was lost.

Nine

$\mathcal{B}$y dinnertime the flood of princesses had slowed to a trickle. Around ten o'clock it stopped. Seventy-nine princesses had come.

Queen Hermione set aside a wing of the castle just for them. Tonight they would sleep in ordinary beds with only one mattress and no pea. Tomorrow the tests would begin. Tomorrow night would be the final exam for those who had passed all the other tests. The mattress and pea test. The test that the Chief Royal Chambermaid was sure nobody could pass.

Prince Nicholas was beside himself.
What was he going to do? And where
was Lorelei?

⚓ ⚓ ⚓

Lorelei was flat on her face in the
forest. She had tripped over a tree root,
and she was too tired to get up. Too tired
to do anything except sneeze.

But she had to get back to the village
and form a search party. She stood and
picked up the picnic basket and blanket.
Her gown and face were covered with
mud and dead leaves. Well, the rain
would clean off her face. And the gown
didn't matter, since she hadn't had a
chance to embroider anything on it yet.

She heard something. She stood still
and fought back a sneeze. There it was
again. A snuffling noise. Trudy! She
opened her mouth to yell. But wait. What

if it wasn't Trudy. What if it was—

Lorelei had never climbed a tree in her life. But she climbed one now. One second she was on the ground. The next she was twelve feet up.

A bear crashed through the bushes. She sneezed. Oh no! He was going to find her!

But he passed right by, in a big hurry. He didn't even look up. He was probably going to his nice warm cave. Lucky bear.

Lorelei climbed down from the tree and stumbled on. "Achoo!" Hang on, Trudy, she thought. Hang on. I'm coming.

⚓ ⚓ ⚓

Nicholas couldn't sleep. He paced up and down in his room. He didn't want to marry anyone but Lorelei. He didn't care about having a princess for a bride. As soon as he married her, Lorelei would be a princess anyway. So what was the difference?

He wouldn't even care that much about becoming a king someday, if Archduke Percy wasn't such a monster.

The wind howled in the forest beyond the moat. He looked out his window. Sheets of rain poured down. Wherever Lorelei had been today, she'd have to be home by now. He wished he could peek in her window and see her, warm and dry and fast asleep, in an embroidered nightgown.

⚓ ⚓ ⚓

Had she seen a light? Way up ahead? So much water was coming down, it was hard to keep her eyes open. "Achoo!"

Lightning flashed, and Lorelei saw a castle. Towers and battlements, dark against the yellow-gray sky.

Who lived there? A royal family? A troll family? Ogres? An evil magician? Maybe she should stay in the forest. "Achoo!" No. She had to go on. For Trudy's sake.

She hurried across the drawbridge. "Achoo!" It would be dry inside. She'd be out of the wind. If the owner was an ogre and he decided to eat her, she'd warm up while she roasted. And if he was a decent ogre, he might even let her take a bath before he cooked her.

She knocked on the thick oak doors. The Chief Royal Night Watchman opened them. A dripping muddy maiden stood there. Another princess? She didn't look like much. But he had his orders, and he let her into the great hall. "Wait here," he barked.

Nicholas had seen the small figure cross the drawbridge. Another one, he

"SHE KNOCKED ON THE THICK OAK DOORS.."

thought. His parents weren't going to like having to get up in the middle of the night for her. He grinned sourly. They'd be sorry they hadn't put in a test for coming in the daytime.

He met his parents on the circular stairway to the great hall where the maiden stood shivering and sneezing.

He couldn't believe it. It was Lorelei! What was she doing here?

Lorelei watched them come down the stairs. They weren't ogres and trolls. One of them even looked familiar. It was that nice Prince Nicholas. Lorelei's heart lurched a little.

She curtsied deeply. She sneezed and wobbled and almost fell over.

They have kind faces, Lorelei thought, but they look annoyed. Except the prince. He looks glad to see me. She sent him a special smile. And then she sneezed.

"Who are you?" King Humphrey boomed. "Which one are you?"

"I am—achoo!—Lorelei. You see—achoo!—I got—"

"Another princess," Nicholas interrupted loudly. "There's always room for one more." He winked at Lorelei, hoping she'd see and go along. Hoping his parents wouldn't see. "Who knows?" he added. "She might be the one to pass the princess tests."

Lorelei saw the wink. He wanted her to pretend to be a princess? She could, if he wanted her to. But why?

She curtsied again. "I am Princess Lorelei. Achoo!"

Ten

"How did you get here?" Queen Hermione asked. "Where's your carriage?"

"Um . . . achoo! Um, I don't have a carriage. Um . . ." What could she say? "Um . . . I . . . I was bewitched." That was it! "Achoo! A fairy put a spell on our whole court. My father was turned into a blacksmith. I became a blacksmith's daughter. I was—achoo!—a baby when it happened."

Quick thinking, Nicholas thought. She was clever, too.

"Absurd! Ridiculous!" King Humphrey roared. "There hasn't been a case or example of a fairy spell in a hundred years. Not since Queen Rosella and King Harold's reign."

"Achoo!"

The lass is crazy, the queen thought.

"Suppose she is a true princess?" Prince Nicholas said. "She might be the only one of the eighty maidens here who is." He hoped Lorelei was paying attention. "If you don't give her the tests, you'll never know. You won't be able to abdicate, Father. I'll never marry. You'll never have grand—"

"Son or heir, you're right." The king put an arm around Nicholas' shoulder. "The boy is correct or accurate."

Lorelei listened between sneezes. Tests? Had they said that if she passed some tests, she could marry Nicholas? Really?

Queen Hermione shrugged. It couldn't do any harm. A true blacksmith's daughter would certainly fail the tests. She rang her bell for the Chief Royal Chambermaid.

"Achoo! Excuse me. My Lady-in-Waiting was with me when we got lost. Achoo! She's still under the spell. She thinks she keeps house for a blacksmith." Lorelei told them about Trudy.

She's so kind! Nicholas thought.

"And our black stallion got lost too. He looks like a mule."

The king called for a groom to ride to the village of Snettering-on-Snoakes to see if Trudy and Leonard had gotten home safely.

Lorelei went upstairs with the Chief Royal Chambermaid. Nicholas followed them. She'll pass one test anyway, he thought, looking at her muddy footprints. She has small feet. But what about the rest?

⚓ ⚓ ⚓

The tests began first thing in the morning.

Lorelei had slept well. Her sheets were satin. The blankets were velvet. The mattress was stuffed with swans' feathers. Just like home. When she woke up, she wasn't even sneezing anymore.

Someone had laid a gown out for her, and a Royal Chambermaid was there to dress her. The gown was pretty, with diamonds sewn into the skirt and pearls sewn into the bodice. But it wasn't embroidered, which was a shame. And look at that! "That's funny," she said out loud.

The Royal Chambermaid curtsied. "What's funny, your ladyship?"

"Well . . ." You'd think they'd get it right for a princess. "The skirt on the gown—I don't mean to criticize—but it's lighter than the bodice."

So Lorelei passed the first test.

Three princesses hadn't noticed. Seventy-seven maidens sat down to breakfast, which was a simple meal. Poached eggs, dry toast, and half a grapefruit—Lorelei's favorite food for breakfast, lunch, and dinner.

While they ate, King Humphrey welcomed them to the kingdom or monarchy of Biddle. Then he explained about the tests, but he didn't say what any of them were. "In closing," he concluded, "let the truest princess conquer or win."

After breakfast, the king and queen and Nicholas gave the princesses and Lorelei a tour of the castle. King Humphrey lectured about Biddle as they went. Nicholas stayed near Lorelei, wishing he could warn her about each test, but the princesses might hear.

When the tour was over, everyone returned to the royal banquet hall for lunch—the next round in the true-princess test (although the contestants didn't know it).

The queen rang her bell, and Royal Serving Maids entered the royal banquet hall.

A salad was placed in front of Lorelei. She picked up her fork.

Now why was a bit of uncooked noodle mixed in with the lettuce? Quietly, she pointed it out to a Royal Serving Maid. And passed the salad test. So that was it, Lorelei thought. You had to guess what was wrong with the food. Funny test.

Five maidens didn't find the noodle. They were escorted out immediately.

Seventy-one to go, Nicholas thought.

He noticed that the crocodile princess was still in the running.

Lorelei found the toothpick under the flounder. It wasn't hard, now that she knew what to look for. Nicholas breathed a sigh of relief.

Only one princess didn't find the toothpick.

Lorelei fished the tiny marshmallow out of her ragout. Eight princesses didn't. One of them was dragged away, yelling, "It isn't fair! Mine melted!"

Nicholas thought he was going to die of worry before the meal ended.

Lorelei found the flake of tuna on the chocolate cake icing. Four princesses didn't. The meal was over. Lorelei and the crocodile princess and fifty-seven other princesses remained in the game.

Eleven

After lunch the measuring began in the queen's bedchamber.

Nicholas and the king weren't allowed to view this part of the test. They waited in the throne room. King Humphrey listened to petitions from his subjects while Nicholas paced up and down, chewing his nails.

In the bedchamber Royal Chambermaids with tape measures checked every inch of every princess. If a princess was too tall, she was out. If she was too short, she was out. If her ears were too big, they were out and she was out.

The measuring took the rest of the day. Lorelei worried about the size of her nose. It was her worst feature. She pulled in her nostrils. When she looked in the mirror, she always thought that made her nose seem a little smaller.

Her nose squeaked by. A hair bigger and she would have had it.

The measuring went on.

The waist of one of the princesses was too big by a sixty-fourth of an inch. Queen Hermione said she was sorry, but if she let this maiden slip by, she wouldn't know where to draw the line.

When the measuring was over, only ten princesses and Lorelei were left. The queen led them to the throne room.

The crocodile princess entered first. Nicholas bit his finger so hard it bled. She smiled at him. Her teeth looked pointy. Where was Lorelei? He held his breath.

Lorelei was the ninth to enter the room. Nicholas started breathing again. They looked at each other. This was scary.

The king gave bouquets to the princesses and congratulated or applauded them on getting so far.

Nicholas wanted to yell, It's another trick! It's a test!

Lorelei held her bouquet away from her to examine it. Some flowers made her sneeze and some made her eyes water. Roses were okay. Daffodils were okay too. Lilies made her sneeze. So did peonies. What was that? Parsley? That wasn't a flower. This was a test! She pulled out the parsley and sneezed.

The bouquet test fooled everyone except the crocodile princess and Lorelei. The best and the worst, Prince

Nicholas thought. He was trembling.

Both of them passed the tapestry test. Lorelei spotted the missing thread from twenty feet away. Nicholas wished she could get extra credit.

King Humphrey announced that they would have a light supper and go to bed. The final test or examination, he lied, would be tomorrow, or the day after today.

Lorelei didn't have a moment to talk privately with Nicholas. She could tell he wanted her to be the one to pass the test, but she wanted to hear him say it. She also wanted him to give her a hint about the big test tomorrow.

He wanted to get near her, too. If he could whisper to her for just one second, he could tell her about the pea. But at supper she sat at the other end of the table, next to the king. Nicholas heard him telling her about his collection of unicorn horns or tusks.

The crocodile princess sat between the king and queen. Nicholas hated the way she ate. She seemed to swallow her food without chewing. And she kept looking at him and licking her lips.

Nicholas excused himself from the table. He went out to the garden and picked up a few large rocks. Then he slipped back into the castle and headed for Lorelei's bedchamber. He'd put the rocks under the top mattress, where she'd be sure to feel them.

But he couldn't get in. The Chief Royal Guard stood in front of the door. Nicholas tried to send him on an errand, but the fellow said that the king had told him not to budge for anyone or any person.

So then Nicholas said he'd leave a note for Princess Lorelei. But the Chief

Royal Guard said, "Begging your pardon, Your Highness, no notes. I have my orders."

Nicholas couldn't do anything. By this time tomorrow either he'd be engaged to Lorelei, or Percival would be the future King of Biddle. Or he'd be engaged to the crocodile princess!

Twelve

Nicholas couldn't sleep. One second he was full of hope. She'd passed all the tests so far! The next second he was in despair. Nobody could feel a pea through all those mattresses. And the crocodile princess had a better chance than Lorelei. After all, the crocodile princess was a real princess, not a blacksmith's daughter.

But it didn't matter. If Lorelei failed, he'd marry her anyway. And his parents would have fits. And Percival would get the throne. He tossed. He turned. He finally slept, and he dreamed of being eaten by crocodiles and drowned in peas.

When Lorelei entered her room, she wondered why her bed had so many mattresses. Last night it had been an ordinary bed. She shrugged. Maybe they wanted her to have an extra-good night's sleep before the big test.

She climbed the ladder and slipped under the sheets. The bed was the softest she'd ever been in. She stretched and wriggled her toes. Mmm. Lovely!

The prince was so nice! Even if he weren't a prince, even if he were a black-smith, she'd love him. But he *was* a prince, and that was even better.

She rolled over. She couldn't get comfortable. The sheets felt all right.

"SHE WONDERED WHY HER BED
HAD SO MANY MATTRESSES."

Satin. Satin was good. The blankets were velvet. Velvet was good.

She closed her eyes.

Something was wrong. Her nose itched and her back ached. She climbed down from the bed and looked at it.

It had to be the mattresses. Maybe there was a pigeon feather in one of them. But which one? There were so many.

She'd never fall asleep. She'd be up all night. Then she wouldn't be at her best for the big test tomorrow. Maybe she could stretch out in front of the fireplace.

She spread a blanket on the floor and laid another one on top of it. Then she got in between them and closed her eyes. The hours crawled by. The floor was hard, but you expected a floor to be uncomfortable. You didn't expect it from a bed piled with twenty mattresses.

Lorelei turned over on her stomach. No better. She rolled back. Could she, Lorelei, actually become a princess? She'd passed every test so far. If she married Prince Nicholas, she'd live in a castle. And so would her father. She giggled. Trudy would be a real lady-in-waiting.

Trudy! She sat up. She'd forgotten to find out if Trudy had gotten home safely. What kind of queen would she make if she couldn't remember her subjects?

She lay down again. She'd ask first thing in the morning. What could the test tomorrow be like? Would they ask her questions? She didn't know any-thing about being a princess. She didn't know much about being a blacksmith's daughter either.

What if they asked her about laws! About geography! About how to sit on a throne! Lorelei was awake all night.

⚓ ⚓ ⚓

In the morning the Chief Royal Chambermaid led the two maidens to the throne room. Lorelei's bones ached, and the skin under her gown was black and blue.

King Humphrey and Queen Hermione and Prince Nicholas were sitting on their thrones. All the courtiers and subjects had been cleared out for the big moment.

The first thing Lorelei wanted to do was to find out about Trudy. Then she'd take whatever test they wanted. She'd probably fail it. But at least she'd know about Trudy.

The other maiden looked so rested

84

and . . . Lorelei hated to admit it, but the other one was beautiful. Maybe by now Nicholas wanted her to win.

"Good morning, princesses or damsels," the king boomed.

"Did you sleep—" the queen began.

"Did you find out—" Lorelei began.

The doors to the throne room burst open. A man rushed in carrying a child in his arms. Lorelei thought the little boy didn't look right.

King Humphrey stood. "What or why—"

"Sire! I am a poor woodcutter! My son is sick, and I have no money to pay a wisewoman to cure him. I have nowhere to turn, except to you."

"Oh dear," Lorelei said. She ran to the child. "Does your forehead pulse?"

The boy nodded.

"Oh dear. Does it hurt to—"

Nicholas interrupted. "If you were a

princess here," he asked the crocodile princess, "what would you do?"

This is the test! Lorelei thought. Maybe the boy wasn't really sick. But he looked sick.

The crocodile princess said, "They should be forbidden to trouble you with their problems. This man and his son must be put to death. That will cure the boy." And she smiled her slow smile.

"What would you do, Princess Lorelei?" Nicholas asked.

What was she supposed to say? Did that horrible one give the right answer? But if you couldn't help people—if you had to *kill* them to make them leave you alone—then she, Lorelei, didn't want to be a princess.

But then she'd have to give Nicholas up.

Well, it didn't matter what the right

answer was. Somebody was sick! "Oh dear. I used to get sick when I was a little—uh—princess. I still do sometimes." She turned to the queen. "Do you have any betony?" Lorelei was sure she was ruining everything, because the queen looked so upset. "I need the leaves of the chaste tree, too. If you don't have that, some bugloss will do. Where's the kitchen?"

Queen Hermione didn't know what to say. So she rang for the Chief Royal Serving Maid.

"Princess Lorelei would be kind to our subjects, Father," Nicholas said, while they waited for the serving maid. "Whether or not she can feel a pea under twenty mattresses." He dropped to his knees so hard, he thought he had broken a kneecap. "Ouch!"

"Oh dear," Lorelei said. A pea?

What was he talking about?

"My darling princess." Nicholas took Lorelei's hand. "Will you marry me?"

"Oh dear. Yes, I'll marry you. We'll need hot water. Does your stomach ache?" she asked the boy.

He nodded.

"Did you sleep or rest well last night, Princess Lorelei?" the king asked. He had to know, even though everything had gotten confused or mixed up.

"No," Lorelei said. "I couldn't get comfortable. So I slept on the floor."

"The pea!" said the queen.

"The pea or bean," said the king.

"Darling!" said the prince.

Epilogue

Lorelei cured the woodcutter's son. King Humphrey and Queen Hermione gave their consent or permission to the marriage of Prince Nicholas and Princess Lorelei.

On their wedding day Nicholas wore a doublet embroidered with parsley, a shirt embroidered with tape measures, and hose embroidered with noodles. Lorelei's hood and veil were embroidered with tuna fish. Her bodice was embroidered with green peas, and her skirt and train were embroidered with tiny mattresses.

Trudy (who was perfectly safe, of

course) was furious that she hadn't gotten rid of Lorelei. But when she moved into the castle, the other Royal Servants showed her the good side of serving a bunch of persnickety monarchs. She learned to agree with them over a dinner of cream of asparagus soup, venison crown roast, and twelve-layer mocha-raspberry cake.

When Sam returned from the earldom of Pildenue, he moved into the palace too. He never understood exactly how Lorelei had become a princess. And he couldn't for the life of him understand why everyone called him Lord Blacksmith. But he liked living in a palace and shoeing the king's wonderful horses.

So they all lived happily ever after.

ALSO BY
Gail Carson Levine

Ella Enchanted

THE PRINCESS TALES:
The Fairy's Mistake
Princess Sonora and the Long Sleep